About the Author

Gavin Catt was born in 1970, and lives outside Melbourne, Australia. He was employed as a clerical officer at a Melbourne hospital, and he is a qualified dental assistant. As a musician, he has played with the Cranbourne Lions Concert Band, the Casey Concert Band and he was the Conductor of the RMIT Concert Band. Gavin enjoys watching science fiction movies, and enjoys books by Suzanne Collins, *The Hunger Games* and David Brin, *The Uplift Series of Novels*. *Sanctuary: Destiny* is Gavin's sixth book.

Sanctuary: Destiny

Gavin Catt

Sanctuary: Destiny

Olympia Publishers
London

www.olympiapublishers.com
OLYMPIA PAPERBACK EDITION

A CIP catalogue record for this title is
available from the British Library.

ISBN: 978-1-83543-112-2

First Published in 2024

Olympia Publishers
Tallis House
2 Tallis Street
London
EC4Y 0AB

Printed in Great Britain

Introduction

It has been twelve months since my uncle, King George passed away, and a lot has happened in the White Commonwealth. Incomplete reports were received by the Council of Crowns that the former Dark Emperor, Mara of Copia had somehow survived the destruction of her prison asteroid by space debris, which was a result of the Sanctuary ordered destruction of a mysterious Kiir freighter that was carrying doom weapons left over from the Dimension War nearly eight years ago, which also resulted in the destruction of the darkship 'Sentinel' because the detonation sequence started twenty-five seconds too early, due to an unknown factor.

I had initiated the explosion as I travelled alone on board the 'Sentinel' out of the Copian system, following Kathryn and Michelle on board the 'Guardian' which was already in interstellar space, for the seventy-minute flight back to Earth.

For months after the Copian mission, I reviewed sensor logs from various sensors in the region where Mara's asteroid was travelling, when I found evidence that a spherical IGAL starship was nearby in the moments before Mara's prison asteroid was destroyed by an Australian Capital Territory sized chunk of the Kiir freighter. The Council of Crowns decided that there was to be a media blackout on the incident, and as king and presiding monarch, I agreed with the decision. We could not take any chances, letting slip that Mara had survived the incident, and then vanished completely.

The Multiverse Council, the Sanctuary Vega Union, and the White Commonwealth had to launch the largest search operation in total secrecy. As the Golden Sceptre in human form, only I could decide Mara's fate, that is, if we could find her and I have discussed this with the members of the White Commonwealth Royal Family in some detail.

Personally, I contacted Link One of 'The Tower' and the mysterious Larip outside our time and they both had agreed that only the Golden Sceptre could decide the former Dark Emperor's fate. I made the decision that when Mara is found, I decided that I will personally execute Mara of Copia. Executions are only carried out when the Council of Crowns has examined the case in detail and only then authorises a death sentence when there is no possibility of mitigating factors, or that the condemned poses a major threat to peace and life in the White Commonwealth.

On a personal level, I was no longer concerned about my eventual merger with the Golden Sceptre. When the time comes, technically I would die, but not in the normal human sense. In my case, it is a transition from my human physicality to becoming a non-physical being. The twist is, I will still be able to communicate in a normal way.

My main projects outside my responsibilities as king and presiding monarch, is to gradually let the beings in the Milky Way know what I have learnt from King George's Dimension War research, and to monitor the first White Commonwealth terraforming project of a planet, which is Project Genesis.

Michelle and I make a joint appearance for the first time on 'Good Morning, Milky Way' to discuss King George's Dimension War research, and the status of the planet Mars as part of what Project Genesis is achieving as the first human led terraforming project. I was relieved that the subject of Mara never came up during the 4D vidscreen interview, and for the last few days, I have reviewed a holo-recording of the interview to make sure that I didn't give any clues that Mara was not dead.

Behind the scenes, I knew that the White Commonwealth Security Service was quietly checking all galactic residents for any clues, no matter how trivial about Mara's location. The only thing that Mara was good at, was disguising herself and because of this, I enlisted the help of a group of beings that have been victims of torture, received from Mara of Copia over the decades.

Personally, I wanted to kill Mara myself, but I said to members of 'The Silent' that if they found Mara first, they could toy with her until I decided when her time ends. In my time with the Shadow, I knew that 'The Silent' would act honourably and do what is required. In the past, I was also a member of 'The Silent' that was tortured by Mara several times before Drago eventually got to me. Instinctively Mara knew that she couldn't kill me as I was more valuable alive to her, plus I did help her to achieve things when it suited me.

Time was advancing, and no matter where Mara hid, I knew that she would be found and that she will receive the justice that she deserves.

Chapter One
Susan

Five years before King George died, my mentor King James also died quite suddenly. No one expected it as King James was in excellent health and was still physically fit despite his advanced years. Both deaths, even though they appeared to be unconnected, were also linked to the death of my father, King Douglas. The thread that connects the three deaths was linked to Mara in different ways.

King Douglas was killed because of his participation in 'The Hunt.' King James died because of an undiagnosed brain aneurism almost too suddenly after a medical check-up and finally, King George's IGAL starship and shuttlecraft being destroyed by a rogue asteroid. All these facts point to one person that was somehow involved, Mara of Copia.

During this time, I made sure that I spent more time with my family, and I was still able to perform my regal duties. However, this seemed to have the opposite effect, I was becoming more stressed, and my anxiety levels rose too, and this was very worrying to me.

I discussed these points with my sister, Kathryn, and Charles. Kathryn gently suggested that I have some counselling sessions with Queen Noor of Andromeda's younger sister, Susan who is an experienced trauma psychologist. Kathryn had given me a strange look, worried that she overstepped the mark, and I assure her that I have been thinking about talking to Princess

Susan, as I had realised that I never worked through my grief about losing three key people in my life in such strange circumstances.

After Kathryn and Charles return home to Centauri after the death of King James, Kathryn gave birth to a daughter, and I was happy for my sister. Kathryn had shown me holo-photos of Bethany, her daughter and I could see the resemblance to Kathryn as I recalled distant memories of when my sister was born, and I remembered that I was three years old at the time.

"King William, are you all right?" I heard Susan ask, bringing my mind back to the present.

I sit facing Susan, and Michelle was sitting next to me. She gives my hand a light reassuring squeeze, and Susan watches me with a sympathetic look on her face and I tell her that my mind has drifted again, recalling the events of the last fifteen years.

Susan says, "You have been through so much over the last fifteen years and I am happy to say that you are making excellent progress, and I know that Michelle is helping you too."

Michelle nods and then she turns to face me and without looking at Susan, she replies to Susan, "This is our journey together. Even the Golden Sceptre needs some help."

After smiling at me, Michelle gives me a kiss, and I give her a sad smile in return.

Susan watches my reaction closely, and Susan says to me, "Michelle's right, sir. The two of you have been through so much together."

After glancing at Michelle. I reply, "You're right, Susan." And slowly my mood and spirits start to lift.

Susan sits quietly, watching me intently, and then she asks me gently, "King William. When you were thinking carefully, a few moments ago and then when I spoke after that, you said that you still grieve the loss of your childhood friend, and colleague in the Galactic Navy, Henry. Am I correct?"

Susan looks at me sympathetically, and so does Michelle when I glance at her.

"It's all right, Will," Michelle says.

"I know that you don't like to talk about this, my love. Just take your time," Michelle adds.

After looking at Michelle, I nod slowly and then I look at Susan, and I start to talk.

Slowly, I talk about the fateful day, when Drago was torturing Henry as he killed him, before Drago turns his attention to me. It was hard to talk about it and I hated every word that I said. Seeing my friend being frozen alive in liquid nitrogen, and in the same way that my father was murdered after 'The Hunt' was almost too difficult to bear.

After Henry's clear walled cell and its frozen contents is dropped from a few metres off the ground, my voice starts to break as I recall the fateful day of my torture, 'From that moment when Henry was dropped, I promised myself that I will have my revenge on Drago and his benefactor, Mara. Drago was told by Rasputin that Mara wanted me for herself.'

I felt utterly alone in the moment, even though Michelle and Susan were right there. A thought occurs to me that Drago has paid for his crimes, and the fact that I was able to convince the Dark Moron that Drago was plotting his adopted mother's downfall, made me feel pleased that Mara's time is ending too.

I look at Susan as she looks at Michelle.

Susan says to me, "Will, you are making excellent progress, how do you feel now?"

Feeling much better, I nod slowly and then I say, "Mara's

time is running out. I know that Mara will be back in custody soon and that I have one final task before Mara is executed."

"What's that?" Michelle asks.

"Mara loves symbolism, and she is going to understand that my face will be the last face that she will ever see," I explain, trying not to laugh.

"That is perfectly understandable," Susan says nodding at me.

"These events are painful for you, but ultimately, your stress levels will reduce after executing Mara, and that you will have fulfilled your regal duties in this situation," Michelle says.

"Thanks for that," I say, thanking my wife in gratitude.

Susan looks closely at me, and she says, "That's all for today, King William. Today has been very painful for you but I am pleased that you are making excellent progress. Are there any questions?" Susan asks with a smile.

"No, Susan. I am grateful for your assistance," I reply as I stand up, looking at a nearby clock. The session started at eight thirty a.m. and it was now ten fifteen a.m.

"Let's go and order a coffee and something light. We may be able to squeeze in an indoor minigolf game or we could adjourn to the lounge area of the informal dining room until lunchtime. It is too hot today to walk in the White Palace grounds," I suggest to Michelle and Susan.

Susan and Michelle exchange a glance and Michelle replies, "Sounds great, my love."

Chapter Two
Morning Tea

After Michelle, Susan and I collect our refreshments from the autochef in the informal dining room. We sit at a nearby table, and we are joined soon after by Rebecca and Marina. Normally, some members of the Royal Family will meet for a main meal, but at other times, our various schedules, normally prevent us from meeting up in the informal dining room. When it does happen, it is very welcome.

I notice Rebecca looking at me and she asks, as I take a tentative sip of my café latte. "How did the session go this morning with Susan, Cousin William?"

Michelle replies, "Your cousin did very well. It was extremely hard for him this morning, Rebecca."

I have another sip of coffee and then say, "Michelle knows that I am a work in progress. These sessions that I am having with Susan, are helping me on so many levels." When I put my coffee mug down on the table, I nod to Rebecca as I know that she understands what I am going through. Rebecca gives me a look of understanding.

Marina asks me, "What do you mean, Your Highness?"

"Firstly, we all know about the issues that I have had with my merger with the Golden Sceptre or to put it another way, my personal destiny. Secondly, as Monarch for trillions of beings in the White Commonwealth and the merger issues that could affect my regal position, and finally, the final shot to be fired in the

White Commonwealth's war with Mara of Copia," I say, lifting my coffee mug to my lips, and I drain what is left of my coffee. Marina stares at me for a moment, and then she nods, indicating that she understood my point.

I look at everyone at the table, "You all realise that I must fire the final shot myself to safeguard the peace and prosperity of this galaxy, as well as the universe. You all know how crucial it is to ensure that peace is maintained."

For a couple of minutes, no one says a word. Instinctively, I knew that they would be curious as to the reasons why I made my previous statement.

"Susan, I have a question for you?" I ask.

Susan looks at me closely. "What is your question, sir?" she replies.

"How about a minigolf game when you come back from Centauri, after our next session. I do concede that I am still stressed to some degree. I thank you and Noor for assisting me. Outside of my own family, I regard you and Noor, Queen Madeira, and Jethro as a part of my own personal cheer squad," I say.

Chapter Three
My Office

After lunch, I remember that I need to attend to some of my administrative work, which includes boxes that I haven't finished sorting through and two that I haven't started yet. When I arrived in my private office, I start working on the government legislation and royal decrees. With a steady rhythm, I finished working through all my boxes in just a couple of hours. I glance at the antique Grandfather's clock that belonged to my father and I note the time; it is now two thirty p.m. I push back the deskpad touchpad, and I sit quietly, I keep my hands on the desk.

On the coffee table, I can see two boxes that I hadn't noticed earlier. "Bugger it," I say quietly, so that the room auto-voice didn't answer. Slowly, I stand up and walk over to the coffee table, sit down on the sofa and I drag the boxes over to me. I open both boxes, and I glance at the contents. I finally remember that Phoebe had placed the two boxes on the coffee table, and that she had told me that the boxes were for the Council of Crowns, and that it wasn't necessary for me to do anything.

Closing the boxes, I glance at the bar in my office, and I decide that I want a drink. I stood up and I go over to the bar, and I put some ice in a highball glass, and I pour some Kahlua over the ice, I add some milk and take my drink over to the desk, stirring the drink. Sitting down at my desk, I have a sip and I start to relax.

My desk comcall unit chimes strangely, and I pick up the

handset. "What is it?" I ask.

"Enigma, Des is on the line for you," Assistant Mansfield replies.

"Please, put Des through, thank you," I say, wondering why Des was using my codename from 'The Shadow.'

"Certainly, sir," Phoebe says, and connects the call.

I hear a series of strange tones. "Enigma, I can confirm that the human woman that I first saw a few months ago, is definitely Mara."

"Did you follow all the procedures for confirming an identity of a target that 'The Shadow' is monitoring?" I ask carefully.

"Yes, King William. She does not suspect that she is under surveillance," Des says in the flat monotone voice that all Cilex use.

"The Silent are sending you their latest information now," Des adds carefully. My screenpad beeps as Des is talking. I read a coded message from 'The Silent' confirming the latest information about Mara.

I run a special coded scan, and it verifies the information that Des has given me.

"Mara is calling herself, Heidi and my regular customers don't like her. She has had a few clients because she comes into the 'Abyss' selling her body. I do know that Mara is staying at 'The Slug' next door," Des explains.

"Des, I will come to Sunev myself, to make casual contact with Mara as the Scrapper to find out what she is planning," I say, knowing what Des's reply will be.

"It could be very risky for you, sir. I will let the stakeout team know that you are coming. Was there anything else, King William?" Des asks in reply.

"I have already sent an e-message to the Zlay, the Shentar

Leadership and the Multiverse Council," I explain.

I hear a screenpad beep on the line, and Des replies, "King William, I am looking at your e-message now. I will pass on this information to the Leader of the Silent, Olaf."

"Des my old friend. Olaf already knows," I explain.

For a moment, I hear only silence. I glance at the comcall unit display, and I can see that the call is still connected.

Des says finally, "You are full of surprises, Enigma. Be careful when you meet up with Mara."

"Thanks, Des, I have something to tell her that will screw with her peanut sized brain," I say. I hear the menacing deep laugh typical of a Cilex.

"Remind me not to piss you off, King William," Des says, with a more human style of laugh, and then we sign off.

After the comcall, I go to the Monarch's apartment so that I can spend quality time with my wife and daughter.

At five p.m., Caroline's babysitter arrives, and my gut instinct tells me that something is wrong. Ever since I arrived in the apartment, I could tell that my daughter was worried about something. Michelle took me aside and tells me that she has asked for Suzi to come earlier, to see if she knows why Caroline has been behaving unusually. Michelle and I talk to Caroline, and we ask her what is wrong.

Michelle and I sit with Caroline and Suzi tells us that Caroline is being teased by an older boy in her class.

I face Caroline. "Caroline, who is saying these nasty things about you?" I ask gently.

"Thomas, Daddy," replies Caroline.

"Caroline, did you say or do anything to upset, Thomas?" I ask, knowing that my daughter was always a gentle soul with others.

"No, Daddy," Caroline answers, looking me in the eye.

I nod slowly, knowing that my daughter is telling me the truth. Glancing at Michelle and Suzi, I could see that Caroline was being truthful with me.

"Suzi, can you please make the appropriate arrangements with Elvira and the school so that Caroline can be home schooled for a few weeks, while this matter is being resolved," I explain.

Suzi replies, "Yes, Your Majesty."

I looked at Michelle. "That's fine with me. What are you going to do now?" Michelle asks. I look at Suzi and she gives me a note with contact details for Thomas's parents, who are both residential White Palace staff.

I pick up my personal comcall unit and ask Assistant Bacon to contact Thomas's parents and ask them to come to the Royal Apartments to see me in our apartment's sitting room.

Turning my attention to Suzi. I say, "Thanks, Suzi. After Caroline's dinner tonight, she can go and play mini golf or watch her favourite 4D vidscreen program."

"Certainly, sir, I know that a couple of her friends are playing tonight," Suzi replies.

Looking at Caroline. I say, "Everything will be all right, and after your dinner, you can have some fun. One of your aunts will be there too, with her daughter, Priya. Priya has wanted to see you for a while anyway. Would you like that?" I ask.

Caroline starts to smile, after being assured that she isn't in trouble. Suzi stands up and holds out her hand, and Caroline takes it. Caroline turns to face me, already looking happier. "Thank you, Father," Caroline says before Suzi guides Caroline from the room.

A few minutes later, after booking a psychological assessment with the White Palace Medical Service for Caroline, two surprised parents and a boy about eleven years old arrive. They are guided into the sitting room of my private apartment, and the family is invited to sit on a sofa opposite Michelle and I.

I explain to Thomas's parents as to why I have summoned them to my apartment.

Both of Thomas's parents face their son. "Thomas, we have spoken to you before about how you treat people at school." Thomas's mother looks closely at me. "We have been aware that Thomas has treated others like this at school. We didn't realise that Caroline is your daughter, Your Majesties."

I look at Thomas directly, and I say, "Thomas, I love my daughter very much and I know that your mum and dad love you. What you did was very wrong, and my daughter will not be at school for a while because of what was said to her," I explain, in a soft, no-nonsense voice.

Looking at Thomas's parents, I ask, "How are things at home?"

"Very tiring and we have a young baby at home now, and my leukaemia has come back, sir," says Thomas's father.

I look at Michelle, who nods at me, suspecting what my response will be.

"You both serve the White Palace, the White Commonwealth, and the royal family well. I know what it is like to be extremely ill too. I am offering you both the chance to relax and refresh on a vacation at Sanctuary. Stay there for as long as you need to and you can come back when you both are relaxed," I say watching the jaws of both of Thomas's parents drop in surprise.

"Thomas, I understand what it is like to have both parents working, as well as a sick parent too. When you return from Sanctuary, that is when your counselling will start. You need to type an apology note and send it to Caroline as soon as you can," I say sternly.

Thomas's parents glance at each other and they say, "Thank you, sir." I thank them for coming, and I said that their leave can start immediately. Both parents and Thomas nod, as they stand to leave.

"Thank you, Your Highness," Thomas says as the family leaves.

"You're welcome," I answer, and Thomas's family leaves the room.

Michelle and I resume talking about our favourite subject, Mara of Copia.

Michelle cocks her head slightly, with a glint in her eye says, "The final round is about to begin, that's great." Despite what Michelle said, I could tell by her tone of voice that she expected more from me.

For a moment, I think carefully.

"I am leaving for Sunev tomorrow, after breakfast so that I can assess the situation, and plan Mara's recapture," I explain.

"Be careful, my love," Michelle replies with concern.

Changing the subject, I say to Michelle, "I found out how Mara escaped that prison asteroid."

Michelle stiffens slightly, and she asks, "How?"

"Do you remember a report from John Hemlock about a strange surface transporter accident and explosion on Mars?" I ask in reply.

"I do, Will," Michelle answers.

"Daron faked his own death in that explosion and escaped Mars, and then subsequently rendezvoused with an associate, and Daron used a Zherk Sphere-ship that was able to get in close enough and beam Mara out," I explained.

Michelle looks at me closely.

"So, what happened to Daron?" Michelle asked.

"Daron was captured by the Zlay, and he was taken back to their own dimension to face justice. Daron isn't Mara's uncle and Rasputin wasn't her father," I say carefully.

"Are you suggesting that Daron was Mara's real father?" Michelle asks with raised eyebrows.

"Bingo, my love. Daron was overheard years ago by a witness at a secret meeting with Mara, Virex, Drago and Gemini," I say with a grin, saving the best to last.

"Who was the witness?" Michelle asks.

"A1 Shentar, who was disguised as a pot plant in the room," I say trying not to laugh at Michelle's shocked expression. "I can't tell you much more as the information is at Quadruple Level Security," I say, which causes Michelle to give me a disappointed look. "I will tell you in an indirect way, without compromising security. The proviso for telling you is please do not ask questions until I have finished. Do you agree?" I ask.

"Yes," Michelle replies, eagerly waiting for my explanation.

For a moment, I think very carefully.

"Daron had been hiding out in the Large Magellanic Cloud in a solar system that is on the opposite side of the cloud that does not face the Milky Way Galaxy. The Sanctuary Vega Union and the Multiverse Council received the news about where the secret meeting between Daron and Mara, was taking place."

"Is that how A1 Shentar overheard the planning in the early stages of the Dark Empire, disguised as a pot plant?" Michelle asks sceptically.

Nodding, I reply, "Sounds like BS doesn't it. As soon as A1 Shentar entered stasis in a pot, his visual receptors and audio receptors continued to function normally. To anyone who didn't know the A1 Shentar was a Shentar, the people that see him wouldn't suspect that A1 Shentar was not a pot plant. In other words, there was nothing unusual about this plant. A1 Shentar was perfectly conscious. It was at this meeting that Mara of Copia formalised her plans for rescue. At this point, Copia was still loyal to the White Kingdom," I explain.

"How does the Golden Sceptre fit into this?" Michelle asks with curiosity.

"This was around the time when the Dark Empire was trying to find the Sceptre. Mara's priority at the time was building her military forces, and this is when Rasputin started to do the bare minimum to assist his daughter. My father, King Douglas was working on a defence plan already for the White Kingdom, assisted by Sanctuary," I explain, not sure if Michelle understood what I meant.

"There is no need to explain this, my love," Michelle says patting my shoulder.

"Thanks, beautiful girl," I say, relieved that Michelle understood my explanation.

"Why don't you come with me to Sunev tomorrow as The Scrapper's wife? You know the profile; besides, we haven't been on a mission together for a long time," I ask unsurely as I forgot if Michelle was busy or not.

Chapter Four
Departure for Sunev

After a good night's sleep, Michelle and I refresh ourselves and then we have breakfast in the sitting room of our apartment and discuss our plans for the meeting with Mara. Caroline joins us for breakfast, and she listens to our conversation.

"Can I come, Daddy?" Caroline asks suddenly, which takes Michelle and I by surprise.

We glance at each other, before I reply.

"You will be spending a couple of days with Aunty Rebecca and Aunty Marina, as they asked if you could stay with them while Mummy and I are away," I answer to a frowning Caroline.

I notice that Caroline is glaring at me in the same way Michelle does when she is unhappy with me. Looking at Michelle, I can see that she is fascinated, and I see a glint of mirth in her eyes.

I turn my chair to face Caroline.

"Caroline, this could be dangerous if you came with us. I wish that you could come, but I cannot allow it. We could be hurt or killed. As king, I cannot allow my heir, to come along," I say seriously.

Caroline starts to cry, and I understood how my daughter was feeling. Many decades ago, when I was about Caroline's age, I experienced these feelings too as my own father had said something like this to me. Michelle gives me a concerned look as I decide how I was going to reply to Caroline.

It was at this moment, that Rebecca and Marina arrive, accompanied by Suzi, the duty babysitter.

"Caroline, could you please come to me," I ask my daughter gently.

Caroline stands, glancing at Michelle, who nods encouragingly and then she faces me. I look into her eyes, and I realised that Caroline thought that she was in trouble. In a pleasant tone of voice, I say, "Sweetheart, I love you more than anything else in the world, and I don't want you to get hurt. In time you will understand why, and you will be a great queen. You're a kind person, just like your mother and father and you will become a better minigolfer than me."

Caroline brightens considerably, after smiling at me, she says, "Yes, Golden Sceptre. I am already a better minigolfer than you." Michelle, Rebecca, Marina, and Suzi start laughing.

My personal comcall unit chimes, much to my relief.

"What is it?" I ask.

"Sorry to bother you, sir. Olaf of The Silent is on the line. He wants you to know that Mara hasn't moved from the Slug, apparently, she is waiting for the Scrapper," Assistant Bacon says.

"Can you advise Olaf to keep watching our friend. If Mara tries to flee, then say that Olaf can do what he likes with the idiot," I say,

"Olaf has said that he will continue to monitor our friend, and deal with Mara, if an opportunity arises," says Assistant Bacon.

Caroline walks over to me. "I am sorry, Father."

"There is no need to apologise or feel sad. Auntie's Rebecca and Marina are looking forward to spending time with you and you are going to have a great time," I say kindly.

Caroline gives me a hug and a kiss, still frowning at me and then she goes over to Michelle, who she gives a kiss and a hug too. Looking at Suzi, Caroline says, "I'm ready." Suzi looks at me, and I nod my assent. Everyone noticed Caroline's discreet snub of me. Before Rebecca, Marina, Suzi, and Caroline leave our sitting room, Caroline looks at me and realises what she did.

"Daddy," Caroline says sheepishly.

"Yes, Caroline," I reply.

"I'm sorry," Caroline says, with tears in her eyes.

I hug Caroline, saying, "It's okay, Sweetie. This happened to me when I was your age, and I do understand how you feel."

I can feel tears in my eyes, which Caroline sees. "I'm sorry, Daddy," she says as she starts to wipe away my tears.

Everyone in our sitting room, watch the discussion closely.

Caroline gives me a smile as she walks over to her aunts. They leave the sitting room, and Michelle and I are alone.

We sit, staring at each other, and then Michelle asks, "Which ship are we taking tomorrow?" I laugh softly,

"We are taking the 'Dog's Breakfast,' after breakfast tomorrow," I answer.

"Why is it called that?" Michelle asks with curiosity.

"It is designed to look like a piece of crap, but it is a state of the art, modern IGAL starship. It just looks like it belongs in a rubbish skip," I reply.

After breakfast the next morning, Michelle and I go to the main White Palace Hangar, Michelle has a strange look on her face as we walk up to the spacecraft, and we stand before the 'Dog's Breakfast.' The look on Michelle's face is priceless.

"Wait until you see the interior," I say as we board the ship. Michelle couldn't help looking at the ship in disgust.

Michelle could see that the ship looked like a children's toy, made with Lego.

We arrived at the doorway to the flightdeck. "Dog's Breakfast, please resume normal internal appearance." And the interior changes to look like an ultra-modern spacecraft. Michelle nods approvingly.

"The Dog's Breakfast is an amazing ship, Will," Michelle says. I smile in return.

"Prepare for Departure," I say clearly.

During the short IGAL flight to the Large Magellanic Cloud, Michelle asks, "How long have you known, Olaf?" Michelle misses nothing, and this is the only thing I never discuss, as this causes me a great deal of pain, even more so than when Henry died. I have never discussed this with anyone at all, and I know that Kathryn, Rebecca, Ann, Elizabeth, and Marina knows. Noor and Susan are the only two people outside the White Commonwealth that know. Strangely though, I am never pressed for answers. As I focus on the transit procedures inside the Large Magellanic Cloud, I can see Michelle waiting patiently as we arrived at the Sunev solar system.

Once we land, I turn to Michelle, and as I shut down the Dog's Breakfast, I tell Michelle about my long-term connection with 'The Silent' and Olaf. I spoke without interruption as we prepared to leave the Dog's Breakfast. When I finish talking, the look on Michelle's face was sympathetic. She realised how distressed I was, Michelle gives me a hug. "Thanks for telling me, my love. I will not press you any more about this."

"Thanks, sweetheart. I wish I could tell you more, but I cannot. This causes me more pain than anything else. I will say that Kathryn knows," I reply, not certain of Michelle's response.

"Thanks, Will. I am sorry," Michelle says, as tears appear.

"Time to get ready," I say, seeing the local time on the

vidscreen near my command chair.

Without a word, we get into the ancient looking surface transporter in the cargo hold of the Dog's Breakfast. The ship lowers the Boarding / Loading ramp and I drive the transporter out of the ship, and I tell the ship that I am clear of the ship.

The ramp retracts as I check the Navigation systems for the best course to the 'Abyss.'

"Game on," is all I say, as we drive a short distance to the 'Abyss' and park in the parking lot at the back. After checking our disguises, which were environment suits, and we leave the surface transporter and enter the Abyss by using a rear entrance.

Michelle knew the reason why I was wearing an environment suit and why, she was wearing one too. Mara has never actually seen the Scrapper's face, and there is a good reason for that. When I first met her as the Scrapper, I told her that my face was severely burnt, when I escaped a burning shuttlecraft that I was fixing in dry dock. I told her that I found out that a certain William Gavin is responsible for my injuries. Despite this, Mara was turned on by this, and she has tried to have sex with me. In typical Scrapper fashion, I told her that she wasn't my type anyway.

Mara giggles like a teenage girl.

"Keep the relationship, business-like. I'm taken!" I snapped. Mara does not suspect duplicity on my part.

Michelle and I make our way into the Abyss, after entering from the rear parking lot. As soon as I see Des, the three of us go into his office and talk there.

"Mara will be here in about one hour from now," Des says, not recognising Michelle at first. The facial expressions of a Cilex are hard to read, and Michelle was standing her ground. Suddenly, Des starts to laugh, which is cut short by Michelle, giving Des the finger. Des apologises to Michelle, and he finishes telling us what we need to know about Mara.

Once we finished talking to Des, we leave his office, and we walk through a maze of corridors and enter the main public area of the Abyss itself.

We sit down at a table, and I check a nearby clock. "Ten minutes until Mara arrives," I say to Michelle on my suit's private intercom system. Michelle nods in response.

Chapter Five
Mara of Copia

The Abyss main public bar was the interior of an old freighter, with the drive engines removed attached to an ancient space station that was never launched. Pastel sunset-coloured walls and a wood panelled ceiling creates an inviting appearance.

Michelle and I didn't have long to wait, sitting at a dingy table, and watching the doorway. Soon enough, a familiar outline appears and Mara slinks across the room to a nearby stage and speaks to the pianist.

The pianist starts to play *Bohemian Rhapsody* by Queen. Mara couldn't see any faces in the crowd, as the stage lights where in her eyes. Dressed in a silver cocktail dress, Mara reminded me of a lighthouse that I saw on Earth.

Mara started to sing, and even I had to admit that she was a great singer. Glancing at Michelle, I could see her nodding. I give Michelle a coded signal to darken her visor, as I knew that Mara would be finishing soon and I could tell that she was happy to see her friend, the Scrapper.

"That cow can actually sing," Michelle says over the private suit to suit intercom.

"You are much better, sweetheart," I reply. Michelle faces me, briefly lightens her suit visor and she gives me a beautiful smile. Then she darkens the visor again and just in time as Mara has finished singing and is on her way to our table.

"Of all the gin joints in the universe, what are you doing

here, Scraps?" Mara says, as she sits down next to me.

"I live here, you moron," I reply and Mara blinks in surprise.

"Nice suit, Scraps. Never to breathe oxygen again. Who's the dame," Mara says.

"Loz is my woman, you know that. She was involved in the accident too. Hence why she is wearing the environment suit. We didn't come here to be insulted, you wanted to see me," I say in the irritated tone that the Scrapper uses, not wanting to appear too friendly.

Mara blinks in surprise again. "I am glad that you and Loz are here, Scrapper," Mara says carefully.

"Here it comes," Michelle says over the suit intercom.

"The Zherk have told me that they helped you," I say to Mara, silencing Michelle. The look on Mara's face indicated surprise. To put her mind at ease, which aided my mission to screw with her mind. I say with care, "Don't worry, no one in the White Commonwealth knows anything about your rescue."

Mara's reaction was strange, she started to massage my groin, in full view of Michelle. I slap Mara's hand away, which makes Mara giggle.

"Sorry, Scrapper. I forgot that you cannot have any fun," Mara says, still laughing.

"When are you getting to the point, Mara?" Michelle asks Mara with annoyance.

"Shut up." Mara snaps back.

"Mara, Loz is my girl, and you will be nice, or else." I snap.

"How is this slimebucket in the sack?" Mara asks.

"You will never find out the answer to that," Michelle says, her tone indicating that Mara should get herself a hobby.

"Come on, Mara. What do you want? My time is money," I say with irritation.

"I have given some thought to your idea, you know, we discussed months ago," Mara explains.

I knew that the plan that Mara was talking about, which is the infamous kidnap plan.

Somehow the Scrapper will work his magic, and kidnap King William, his wife and sister. As the Scrapper, I weaved together such a complex plot, I wanted to keep Mara from guessing the true purpose of the plan, and that is for her to be bamboozled and to discourage her from considering using the plan.

"It's an insane plan, Scraps, but I cannot wait until I catch up with King William and his wife in particular," Mara says.

"Why her?" I ask, looking at Michelle's darkened visor.

"I want her dead," Mara says ominously. Michelle says to me on the private suit to suit intercom.

"She hasn't forgotten what I did with her laser pistol," Michelle replies.

"Don't worry, my love. Mara will pay for her crimes," I answer Michelle.

"What are you two crapping on about?" Mara asks, becoming suspicious because she couldn't hear what Michelle and I were talking about.

"Loz was just telling me in her own language, what King William did to her," I explained.

"He tortured me and threatened me with exile," Michelle explains.

Mara nodded with fake concern, and replied, "We will kill William together."

I look at Mara closely and I say, "I agree, so let's meet at the Crypt and we can get the ball rolling." This grabbed Mara's attention immediately.

"You can make this plan work, Scraps," Mara says eagerly.

"Of course, I will engage some of my resources from Pavlov's Rim," I say enigmatically.

Mara was now behaving like an excited puppy. "So when do you want to meet at the Crypt?" Mara asks.

Looking at Michelle's darkened visor, I reply, "Give me at least seven days."

Mara nods, and answers, "One week it is."

Mara stands up and walks away from our table, trying to offer personal services as she heads towards the exit. Without getting a customer, she leaves the 'Abyss' without a word.

Michelle and I immediately lighten our visors as Des comes over to our table, and we discuss my plan (the Scrapper's) and with nothing else to discuss, Michelle and I return to the 'Dog's Breakfast,' and we depart immediately for Earth.

Chapter Six
Earth

On our return to Earth, Michelle and I go to our apartment, and discuss plans for what will happen next. As the Scrapper, I had told Mara that I would kidnap Michelle and Kathryn. Fortunately, Kathryn, Charles and their daughter Bethany would be coming to Earth in the next few days, and I knew that every senior member of the royal family understands that the kidnapping plan would not occur, and they all agreed to give me their full co-operation.

At dinner that night, Michelle expressed her dislike of the kidnap idea.

"Your idea is too risky, Will. I don't like it at all," Michelle says, with her fork pointing at me.

Looking at my wife, I answer, "You need to understand that the kidnapping will not actually take place, because if it did, Mara would put two and two together. The Scrapper will tell Mara that the White Commonwealth has upgraded security, which makes the kidnaping impossible."

Michelle still looked confused, and I add, "If you are having trouble understanding this, what about Mara."

"Smoke and mirrors?" Michelle asked.

"That's correct," I reply, nodding.

"So, this is what you meant when you said that you are screwing with Mara of Copia's peanut sized brain?" Michelle answers.

"Only a small part, sweetheart. The beauty of this is that Mara is screwing with her own mind too, and she doesn't realise it," I explain.

Two days later, Kathryn, Charles and Bethany arrive on Earth, and Michelle and I greet them in the White Palace Hangar. I ask Kathryn and Charles to join Michelle and I, once they have settled in. I summon Rebecca, Marina, Ann, Elizabeth, Albert, George, and Edward to my apartment, as there is much to discuss. It was fortunate that the Council of Crowns had a meeting scheduled for a couple of days from now.

Briefly, I discuss my plans and there was understandable shock. If I weren't king, I would be stunned too. I explain that the final act is about to begin, and I ask everyone to trust my instincts, and I remind them that it is my duty to punish Mara. Rebecca and Marina look at each other and they face me, nodding their agreement, quickly followed by the others.

"You all understand that I wish that what I have to do to Mara wasn't necessary," I say sighing. The others exchange glances, and then they face me.

"We understand, Golden Sceptre," Michelle says. The others watch me closely, nodding sympathetically. Everyone knew that the stakes were high, and that I was struggling with my feelings.

Using the screenpad that I use for my messages as 'The Scrapper,' I send an e-message to Mara saying that the kidnap plan will not work and I assure her that when I get to the Crypt, I will have thought of something more diabolical. Within a minute of sending the e-message, Mara replies, and I glance at the others, and I read Mara's reply.

"Mara has replied to the message that I have just sent," I announce.

"You need to scarper, Scrapper. The White Commonwealth

must be onto you. Meet me at the Crypt if you can get away, and I will protect you," I explain the contents of Mara's reply, and then I look at everyone in the room and I saw looks of concern and curiosity.

I stand up and I walk over to the autochef in my apartment, with every eye watching me. After removing the café latte that I ordered and I sit back down where I was, and I have a quick sip of coffee. Briefly, I close my eyes, savouring the flavour of my coffee before I resume speaking.

"The latest intelligence report we have is that there are only fifty people that are still loyal to Mara, and they are responsible for security at the Crypt. The Silent have advised me that the Crypt is being prepared now for Mara's return," I explain. Kathryn who had been silent for a while asks,

"When is Mara's expected return to the Crypt?"

"Within the next forty-eight hours. Des has added that Mara has left The Slug, and she has boarded her IGAL Star Yacht," I reply.

Kathryn nods in agreement.

"What are conditions like at the Crypt, at the moment, cousin?" Marina asks.

"Typical of empire remnants that are not absorbed by the White Commonwealth. Supplies are running short and due to the rust bucket nature of the Crypt; morale is exceptionally low. It is only a matter of time before Mara's loyalists defect. The Zlay, the Shadow and the Silent are monitoring all possible escape routes. I know that the Zherk are monitoring too, as well as communicating with the Sanctuary Vega Union and the Multiverse Council."

Kathryn and Marina exchange a quick look, before I add, "The final round is about to begin."

"Why don't you just catch Mara now?" Charles asks irritably.

"Lives could be lost, Charles," Kathryn replies looking at me for confirmation.

"We are going to toy with her first, and once we are ready, we will strike," I explain to Charles, realising that Charles's question was reasonable.

"I do know that Mara's rebel forces have planned to place bioweapons containing Niataxis developed by Drago years ago, in strategic locations throughout the White Commonwealth," I say, trying to explain in an indirect way, why a direct assault to extract Mara from her hideout wouldn't work.

"What?" Kathryn exclaims.

I stand up and I walk over to a secure cabinet, unlock it with a special key, take out a small briefcase and I carry it carefully over to the coffee table. I open the briefcase so everyone could see the contents. Every single person in the room gasps when they see the contents. Ten clear glass vials containing a clear fluid sit in padding.

"The Shadow obtained this briefcase from its hiding place, in a storeroom at the Crypt several weeks ago and passed this onto me. These vials are the ones that vanished decades ago, squirreled away by Daron for a rainy day. All other vials were found, and they have been destroyed. Mara still thinks that she has them, but the vials she does has contain only water," I explain.

A1 Shentar enters the room, and I hand the case to his assistant. "These vials will now be destroyed," A1 Shentar's assistant explains. The assistant places the case inside a device that resembles a microwave oven.

The assistant enters some numbers and touches the device's

'Activate' icon, and then we hear a muffled boom. The assistant opens the device and there are only ashes.

"All done, King William," the assistant says.

And A1 Shentar adds, "We can all relax now." I nod to my friend and Leader of Sanctuary, knowing that A1 is not due to leave for a few hours.

Later at lunch in the informal dining room, A1 Shentar joins the family, sitting on a Shentar chair and joins in on the casual discussions at the table. The regular lunchtime crowd pays no attention to us.

"How is the recovery operation going, Will?" A1 Shentar says quietly to me, as I notice several of his visual receptors watching the others at the table in an engrossing conversation on minigolf champions.

"We will have her soon. Apparently, what's left of Mara's loyalists have received an offer that they cannot refuse, which is to get arrested or co-operate with us. Olaf of the Silent made the offer to them, my friend," I reply.

A1 Shentar flutes a note of surprise, then says, "Fair enough. When will Mara be in custody?"

I look at a nearby wall clock, "The Silent will capture Mara in the next few hours. The recovery operation was started as soon as she left Sunev," I explain.

I notice that Kathryn had heard my conversation with A1 Shentar, and she nods in our direction. "Why didn't you tell us that?" Charles exclaims in a questioning tone of voice.

A1 Shentar could tell that I was starting to become annoyed with Charles again, so he answers, "Only the Golden Sceptre can decide what happens with information like this."

"I told you that, Charles," Kathryn says.

Michelle had been silent during the conversation so far, but now glares at Charles and I say, "I know that you don't understand much about the complexities of the recovery operation, and that's OK. However, you will be continuing your follow up counselling after the CovZlay treatment, Prince Charles. That is an order."

Charles appears to think about what he said, and he says to me, "King William, I am very sorry." Rebecca is looking at me and I nod slowly. Rebecca notes down the incident with Charles, on her screenpad and looks at me questioningly. I nod again, giving my consent for Rebecca to proceed, and I can tell that she sent a report to the White Palace Medical Service, and to Princess Susan of Andromeda.

"Mara should be arriving at the Crypt soon. So, it shouldn't be too much longer before we have her in custody," I say, looking again at the nearby wall clock.

Everyone at the table looked surprised.

"How do you know that my love?" Michelle asks.

"Olaf has just sent me a coded message," I say, looking at my screenpad. "Mara is in her clapped out, rust bucket, IGAL Star Yacht, which she had to borrow from a friend," I say, trying not to laugh.

"The Scrapper strikes again," Kathryn says with a grin.

"Apparently, her ship had a fault that the Scrapper couldn't fix quickly, so she has borrowed an old ship that has been at the Shez Nez shipyards for years," I reply laughing.

A1 Shentar stands to leave, and I offer to accompany him to his IGAL ship. He assures me that it wasn't necessary and says, "I will see you at Sanctuary soon, King William. Keep me posted on the latest with Mara."

"OK, A1. See you soon," I reply, nodding and A1 Shentar leaves the informal dining room.

After the Leader of Sanctuary leaves the informal dining room, there was little to do except return to our duties. We cannot do anything about Mara until she has been detained.

Chapter Seven
The Zherk

Ever since we found out that Mara had escaped her prison asteroid, I wondered who in their right mind would want to help her. I knew that the Zherk worked with the Dark Empire, and somehow Mara has had access to Zherk technology, which freed her. The White Kingdom knew that Mara would have convinced the Zherk that we were the bad guys. A1 Shentar had confirmed to me that the Zherk were blind sighted in the same way that the Zlay were, however Sanctuary did not have direct contact with the Zherk until recently.

Not even the Multiverse Council had easy access to information about contacting the Zherk in our Dimension, but we did know that they wanted to have peaceful and productive relations with the White Commonwealth.

The next day, Kathryn, Charles, Michelle, Rebecca, and Marina were enjoying an early lunch when my sister asks logically, "Have you considered asking the Larip outside our time, about our dilemma." And for a moment, I stare at my empty plate, thinking carefully, and then I look at my sister.

"I have contacted the Larip outside our time, and I was advised that 'The Tower' have contacted the Zherk, and the Tower have advised me that the Zherk will contact the White Commonwealth and the Larip has assured me that the Zherk have a code of conduct, which is not unlike the Zlay or the Shadow. The Zherk were jealous that the physical Golden Sceptre never appeared in their dimension," I explain, looking at everyone at the table.

Michelle gives me a concerned look, but for the moment, she says nothing.

Marina looks like she is going to ask me a question when I see her facial expression change. She nods at me in the direction of the main informal dining room doors, and I turn my head slightly and I see Admiral M entering the dining room. Admiral M sees me looking and he comes straight over, acknowledging the others who were watching closely.

Admiral M stands next to my chair, as I turn to face him. I indicate that it is OK for him to sit down on the chair next to me, which seems to annoy Charles, so I shoot him a very annoyed look, before I focus my attention on Admiral M.

Admiral M sits down, saying to me, "I am sorry to disturb you, sir. Ten Zherk Sphereships have emerged from Stanton's Void, and Queen Noor of Andromeda have asked us to let you know. According to Freedom Hall, the Zherk Sphereships are heading our way." And then Admiral M falls silent.

This interests me because when the Zherk enter our universe normally, they normally enter near Vega.

Admiral M's comcall unit chimes. He holds it like a telephone handset and before I even knew what is going on, the comcall is over. "That was the Head of the White Commonwealth Security Service, sir. The Sanctuary Vega Union has received a formal request from the Zherk Fleet Commander. The Zherk Praetor wishes to speak with you personally and the Zherk Praetor assures me that their intentions are peaceful," Admiral M says, looking at me.

"What do you think, Will?" Kathryn asks.

Thinking carefully. I reply, "I am sure that the sentiments are genuine," I answer my sister. "Admiral, could you please advise the Sanctuary Vega Union, that I am happy to talk to the Zherk, however, I do need the Zherk to follow all instructions given by Galactic Space Traffic Control," I say to Admiral M who nods slowly in understanding.

Admiral M relays my request to the Sanctuary Vega Union, and he says to me, "King William. The Zherk Praetor accepts our terms, and the Praetor will comcall you directly."

My personal comcall unit chimes and I answer, "Go ahead, Aisha."

"King William, Praetor Augustus of the Zherk, is on the line," my Assistant Aisha replies.

"Thanks, Aisha. You can put him through," I ask, and I hear the connection chime beeping once.

"This is King William," I say cautiously.

"This is Praetor Augustus of the Zherk. We need to talk in person, as I have information that is relevant to you. I am aware that you are suspicious of the Zherk, but I want to assure you, your majesty, that the Zherk Empire was misled by the person that you call the Dark Emperor, and now, it is a matter of honour that the Zherk wants to right the wrongs of the past, and we desire a positive relationship with the White Commonwealth," says the deep voice of the Zherk Praetor.

I ask the Zherk Praetor to give me a moment to think, which he agrees to without question. I look at everyone, and I explain the comcall so far.

"It's the same set of circumstances as it was with the Zlay, Will," Kathryn comments, with the other members of the family, nodding.

"Thanks, Kathryn," I reply, and I reconnect the call, apologising to Praetor Augustus for the delay.

"That's OK, King William," Praetor Augustus answers, and we make the necessary arrangements for the arrival of the Zherk Delegation.

Two hours later, all ten Zherk Sphereships enter the solar system and they enter orbit around the sun, between the Earth and Mars. Closely watching the arriving Zherk fleet, was a Sanctuary Vega Union IGAL starship, Sanctuary Security, and the White Commonwealth's own Galactic Navy flagship, the Australis.

A few minutes after the arrival of the Zherk fleet, a small Zherk shuttlecraft leaves one of the Zherk Sphereships and it flies escorted to Earth.

Michelle and I go to the White Palace Spaceport to meet the arrival of the Zherk Shuttlecraft and we arrive a couple of minutes before the shuttlecraft is due to arrive. We stand next to the surface transporter as we see looking up and in front of us, the Zherk shuttlecraft descending towards the landing pad. Silently, the shuttlecraft lands with its tricycle landing skids deployed, and moments after touchdown, a boarding ramp extends out and down, and three Jek humans walk down the ramp, with two in coveralls behind the Praetor who was dressed smart casually in a blue polo shirt and black jeans. The Praetor walks towards us as we start to move forward towards our visitors fifty metres away.

"Welcome to Earth, Praetor Augustus," I say, looking at the Praetor, who appeared to be about thirty years old.

"Thank you, King William," Praetor Augustus replies. "And my assistants, Shari and Seetar," Praetor Augustus says. Shari nods to me and then I look at Seetar, and I was shocked. It was the Seetar that nearly triggered an interstellar war.

It was strange to see a subdued looking Seetar, and I sensed

Michelle tense up, when she realised that this is the trouble causing Seetar from Sanctuary.

The Zherk party accompanies Michelle and I back to our surface transport, and we enter the vehicle and sit down, and then the surface transporter moves away. Inside the surface transporter, both parties talk casually for the next couple of minutes as the surface transporter travels the short distance back to the White Palace complex and we stop at the entry doors to the Administration wing of the White Palace.

We head inside, and we go straight to my private office sitting room and we sit down on the sofas.

"How can the White Commonwealth assist you, Praetor Augustus?" I ask.

"I can confirm that the human woman that you know as Mara of Copia, actively worked to discredit you and your father, King William, assisted by her father, Rasputin and I am ashamed to say, my own father who believed those lies. Consequently, my father assisted the Dark Emperor, to put you in custody, and press your ship, the Australis into service with the Empire Navy. The Zherk Empire wants to correct the wrongs of the past, as we realised too late, Mara's true intentions. The Zherk government understands that you may not trust us," Praetor Augustus explains.

"Are you aware that I know Seetar? He betrayed the Tower and actively tried to sabotage the work of Sanctuary," I explained, glaring at Seetar, who appeared to be in a daze.

"The Zherk Empire wants to assure you that Seetar is under our control now, and we will understand if you do not trust us. The parts of Seetar's brain that are responsible for his crimes, were removed, but he retains the memories of what he did," Praetor Augustus says.

"I am sorry, King William," Seetar says in a flat monotone voice.

Praetor Augustus says, "We will understand if you do not want Seetar present."

"He can stay, Praetor Augustus," I answer.

"Seetar, you have betrayed your Delegation and me at Sanctuary in the past. I will allow you to remain, so that you can do your job. You deserve to be punished, Seetar. If you step out of line while you are here, you will be locked up," I say, pointing at Seetar.

I realised that the psychological controls being used on Seetar, must be extraordinarily strong and I knew that I needed to get back on track.

I wanted a more detailed explanation of Augustus's connection to Mara, so without beating around the bush, I ask, "Augustus, what is the connection between Mara and the Zherk?"

"As you know so far, Mara was able to convince my predecessor, who by the way was my father, before Mara thought that he was becoming inconvenient, she found him quite useful. We actively tried at one stage, to kill both you and your father, but many in the Zherk High Council realised that Mara and her father were liars and that the White Kingdom was acting with honour. We knew that you weren't perfect, but who is perfect. Our Empire isn't perfect. Mara and Rasputin had forgotten Daron, to his advantage," Praetor Augustus explains.

Michelle looks at me and I return her look as we both had forgotten about Daron's role in Mara's rescue from the prison asteroid.

"What about King William's relationship with various intergalactic and multiverse organisations?" Michelle asks looking straight at Augustus.

"Do you mean, how did we sort the sheep from the goats, Queen Michelle?" Praetor Augustus asks.

Michelle nods her head. "That's right," she replies.

"News about what your husband did for the Katarie and others in the multiverse, spread throughout the multiverse. Your husband made many friends long before there was any consideration of allowing the White Kingdom into Sanctuary. He became well known throughout the multiverse, long before the White Kingdom joined Sanctuary, for his knowledge, and we understood why he personally didn't trust the Zherk Empire for so long," Praetor Augustus explained, looking at the time. It is now three p.m., which is on the clockface of my father's antique Grandfather's clock nearby.

"The Zherk Empire is looking forward to hearing, about Mara's imminent arrest. I wish you well with that, your highness," Augustus says.

"This time, there is no escape for Mara," I reply.

Praetor Augustus nods in agreement and his two colleagues take notes, and I can't help staring at Seetar. Even though Augustus assured me that Seetar was under control, I still didn't trust Seetar. Glancing at Michelle, I see her watching the two assistants, and I knew that Michelle didn't trust our dear friend Seetar either. Despite all this, I could sense that there has been a change in the former Delegate to Sanctuary for the Tower, and now isn't the time to ask for details.

I explain to Praetor Augustus of the Zherk, what will happen to Mara of Copia once she is in custody, and once I have carried out her execution, the final stage of the destruction of the Dark Empire will be complete.

"Mara deserves death, King William, and I know that this is a cross that you have to bear," Praetor Augustus comments. I nod my head curtly, because I am waiting for an explanation of how Mara was able to be rescued from her prison asteroid.

"Mara was able to escape her confinement because the Zherk shuttlecraft was able to lock in on Mara's position, and the high-speed transport beam engaged. These shuttlecraft are normally used by our emergency services, and the one that Daron was using, was stolen months before by the Karshid Clan. I do understand that Sanctuary uses similar technology as well as the White Commonwealth," Augustus explains.

"Absolutely correct," I answer.

Out of the corner of my eye, I can see that Michelle is watching me. As I turn to face her, Michelle asks, "Are you all right, my love?"

"All good. Thanks, sweetheart," I reply.

"Praetor Augustus, let's work together to trap Mara, and then we can talk further on developing new trade opportunities for the White Commonwealth and the Zherk Empire?" I say keenly, and then I add, "Would you like to stay for dinner, Augustus?"

"Sorry, King William. I need to return to my ship," Augustus replies.

We both stand up and shake each other's hands in farewell and without looking at his assistants, Praetor Augustus leaves my private office.

Despite my earlier misgivings, I knew that I could trust Praetor Augustus of the Zherk.

The screenpad that I use for my communications as Enigma, beeps suddenly. I type an e-message in reply, telling Mara that the Shadow cannot assist her and that the White Commonwealth was also breathing down my neck, which makes direct assistance impossible.

Mara replied immediately, "I think that the Golden Sceptre

will destroy us both."

For a moment, I think very carefully, because I knew that Mara wasn't stupid. I start typing on the screen-pad for Enigma. *"I am going to make myself scarce for a while, and I will help you as soon as I can. I have let the Scrapper know to make himself scarce too."* And I sign off by sending the e-message.

And Mara's reply is immediate, *"Fair enough, I am meeting the Scrapper at Pavlov's Rim. He was supposed to meet me at the Crypt, but he told me that the heat was on. Take care."* And Mara signs off the e-message.

I look at Michelle and I say, "Mara's final act is about to begin."

Michelle looks at me closely. "How much longer?" Michelle asks.

"Only a few hours from now," I reply, noticing Michelle's smile.

"What?" I ask.

"Your dedication is the reason why this operation is working, Will, and I thank you for your hard work," Michelle says sincerely.

"Thanks, sweetheart. Everyone has played their part very well, and without the backup, Mara would still be running most of this galaxy."

I look at a nearby clock, and Michelle follows my gaze. We both nod, knowing what needs to happen next.

Chapter Eight
The Scrapper

After my audience with the Zherk Praetor, Michelle and I join Kathryn and Charles, as well as Rebecca and Marina for dinner in the informal dining room. Halfway through dinner, my personal comcall unit chimes unexpectedly.

I take the unit out of my polo shirt pocket, "What is it?" I ask, slightly annoyed at the interruption, and the conversations at the table stop immediately.

"I am sorry to disturb you, sir, but you asked to be told when the Zherk Sphereships left the solar system, and they will be exiting the galaxy in nearly one hour from now," the royal security officer said.

"Thanks for letting me know," I reply.

Before I had a chance to relax, and resume chatting with the others, the screenpad that I use for my Scrapper communications, beeps suddenly. "Shit." I swear, under my breath. Looking at my sister, I see the ghost of a smile, and I noticed that Michelle was looking straight at me too.

After reading the e-message, I look at everyone and I say, "This message was from you know who. Mara is going straight to Pavlov's Rim as we speak. She says that she needs the Scrapper's help after all."

Michelle gives me a quizzical look. "It is so sad that she has no more friends now. What do you intend to do, Will?" Michelle asks.

"Mara already knows how to get to Pavlov's Rim, and she will be consolidating the resources that she has left, with the Scrapper," I answer and then I start laughing.

"What are you not saying?" Kathryn asks.

"Mara will be captured after she arrives at Pavlov's Rim."

Pavlov's Rim is a solar system that is orbited by several black holes, and a super massive white hole. Before an IGAL Starship makes the trip to Pavlov's Rim, a very precise course needs to have been programmed into the NAV systems, and few human pilots have ever flown there. My father had given me the keys to everything about Pavlov's Rim so that I would be perfectly safe entering and leaving the solar system and there is an asteroid field that fills the solar system which makes navigation tricky.

I look at a nearby clock. "The recovery operation has started," I say.

"It is the final roll of the dice for Mara of Copia," Michelle says smiling and we finish our meal.

As soon as the evening meal is finished, coffee is served and the chatting resumes.

This time, the Scrappers screenpad beeps, and I read a short e-message from Mara.

"You're the best, Scraps, Mara."

I look at Michelle and Kathryn, who look at me expectantly.

"You know who has arrived at the Rim," I say carefully.

A look passes between my sister and wife, and Kathryn asks me, watched by everyone at the table. "When is Dopey being detained?" I hold my left hand up, silently asking for everyone to give me a moment.

I take my personal comcall unit out of my polo shirt pocket and I enter a special code into the keypad. Seconds later, I hear the voice of Olaf, Leader of the Silent.

"It's me. You are clear to detain our friend. I will leave the method up to you. If she resists, accidents may happen but if not, could you please persuade Mara to join me. I will let Admiral M know. Enigma out," I say to Olaf who is laughing.

"No problem, Enigma. Will do. She will be detained very soon, we are watching her now and we have deactivated her ship's systems remotely as per your instructions," Olaf explains.

"Thanks, mate. I owe you a drink and a minigolf game," I reply.

"Thanks for everything, King William," Olaf replies.

"Catch you soon," I say, signing off.

"What are you smiling about, cousin?" Rebecca asks me.

"We will have Mara in custody within the hour, and Admiral M knows what to do next," I say, typing on my own screenpad and sending the message to Admiral M.

"Well done, sir." I hear from Charles who was obviously still sulking after I told him off recently. I nod in thanks to Charles and everyone at the table.

"I need a drink, feel free to join me," I say as I finish my coffee and I sit thinking carefully.

"Time will tell, how well the process went that was used to detain Mara of Copia," I say eventually, and I watch the others glance at each other.

"What do you mean, Will?" Michelle asks.

"We all know that Mara has the personality and charisma of a house brick, and we also know that she is not completely stupid either. Mara will experience a slightly different form of her special treatment that she has had before. This time, I am allowing her to speak when she joins me in my office, but she will not be told that she can talk, until the time is right," I explain.

"I can't help feeling sorry for her," Kathryn says laughing. For some unknown reason, Kathryn's laughter annoyed me.

"Mara has killed millions of beings and I don't think that this is a laughing matter, Queen Kathryn, as I will be executing her personally, and you know that it is my duty." And I stand up glaring at Kathryn and I walk out wordlessly to the outside doors to the inner courtyard between the Royal apartments wing, Administration and Staff apartments wing of the White Palace.

I was so angry at myself for the way that I spoke to my sister, and I knew that she understood the pressures that I am under, and I think as I walk around the courtyard in the early evening. The sun wasn't due to set for several hours as it is November, and the first warm night of the spring. Winter is always very mild and the cold and wet conditions back in the 21st Century changed due to climate change, driven by self-serving interests that claimed that their recyclable renewable energy generators cared for the environment, but research found that green power to be more wasteful. Fusion and vacuum energy now provides base load power. Solar power is now much more efficient than in the 21st Century thanks to now non-biased scientific research.

These things, I was thinking of when I was eventually found by Rebecca and Marina. I was sitting at a picnic table when I saw Rebecca and Marina approach. I motion that it is OK for them to sit down, and they seemed to hesitate.

"Please sit down, your king needs your help," I say, looking at both cousins who nod and they sit down with me, patiently waiting for me to speak. Slowly at first, I say that I knew that Kathryn was joking but I was concerned that I was treating the situation too seriously and I asked them what they thought.

Rebecca and Marina look at each other and then Rebecca says, "Cousin, you have proven to all of us many times that you take your role as king seriously. We understand that being the Golden Sceptre has changed you, cousin. You just need to be more patient than ever before, when dealing with others and work to relax your mind.”

“Is Kathryn mad at me?” I ask.

“Annoyed, yes but she knows that you must maintain your guard. Kathryn acknowledges that it is difficult for you to relax,” Marina says gently.

“Where is Kathryn now?” I ask my cousins.

“Kathryn is in the lounge area of the informal dining room,” Rebecca replies.

I walk back to the informal dining room accompanied by Rebecca, Marina and my Royal Guard Detail and I look at Kathryn as I entered the Lounge area. The fact that I could see that Kathryn had been crying upset me and I watch Michelle and Kathryn tense up slightly as I sit down opposite them.

Before I have a chance to say anything to my sister, Charles comes up to me and pours his drink over my head and throws his empty glass that hits me on my right shoulder and shatters all over me. “Screw you.” Charles snarls at me and I look at my Royal Guard Personal Security team and I give them a coded nod. The security team comes over and detains Charles.

“Confine him to his quarters, until I say otherwise,” I say in a shaken voice as Charles is taken away and I look at Kathryn and Michelle who watched the whole exchange.

Room Attendants come to clear up the mess and I focus on my wife and sister.

“Kathryn, I wish to apologise for my attitude this evening. I should have understood that you were joking about Mara. This was a perfect example of what happens if you get too focused on something for so long, and you forget those that support you,” I say in an apologetic tone.

At first, Kathryn just glares at me, and then I detected a change in her facial expression.

"Will, I should be apologising to you. I never intended to hurt you and I know that duty is important to you, and I thank you for everything that you do," Kathryn says looking at me.

"You are welcome, Kathryn. Do you want another drink?" I ask.

"No thanks, Will. Why don't we watch a 4D vidscreen comedy film? We both need a laugh," Kathryn says.

"You're on," I say with a smile. I look at a nearby Royal Guard,

"Prince Charles can be released, no charges needed," I say.

"Thanks, Will. Charles has been a pain again," Kathryn says.

"We will sort it out," I reply.

The look on Kathryn's face was happier, when I find a 4D vidscreen movie that I knew that Kathryn would like, "How about this one?" I ask, looking at Kathryn and the others. Kathryn looks at the movie description, and the others were looking too.

"Looks good, Will," Kathryn says as Charles returns. The atmosphere changed dramatically as everyone watches Charles stand in front of me.

"Prince Charles, if you ever disrespect me like that again, ever. Watch out. Until your vacation period ends in a couple of weeks, you are suspended. No ifs or buts. You are not allowed to leave the White Palace Zone; however, your administrative duties must be carried out as normal," I state, glaring at Charles.

"I am sorry, sir," Charles says like a petulant kid.

I stand up, facing Charles. "You can stay here to watch the movie," I say, and I sit down next to Michelle. "Start playback," I say to the 4D vidscreen.

After the vidscreen movie finished, everyone decides to retire for the evening. I was still angry with Charles, and Michelle could tell the recent incident with Charles, was still on my mind. Michelle and I acknowledge everyone as we leave the lounge area, and Charles glares at me as we pass him and Kathryn. The look on Kathryn's face was a concern, and I wondered what really triggered Charles's attack on me.

Michelle and I say nothing about the subject as we walk to our apartment, and I knew that we both needed to cheer each other up, so I suggest that we check up on Caroline, who should be asleep. Michelle's face brightens at my suggestion, and I enter our apartment, and we go into Caroline's room. In the glow of the night light, we can see that Caroline is asleep, lying on her side facing the door. Michelle kisses Caroline on the forehead, and Caroline murmurs something in her sleep, and then I kiss Caroline on the forehead as well, and Caroline smiles in her sleep.

Michelle and I return to our bedroom, and we quickly refresh and change for bed.

Michelle and I lie down, facing each other and we quietly chat. Michelle was genuinely concerned by what happened with Charles.

I say to her, "I will talk to her alone, and find out what is going on with Charles."

"Charles may have been concerned that you upset Kathryn, when you told her off," Michelle says looking into my eyes.

"I understand that, my love. Kathryn and I have worked together for so long in the field, we were using a code when she made that comment earlier and then I responded, by 'expressing my concern' afterwards," I explained cryptically.

Michelle stares at me closely when she replies, "You said a

code. Now I get you, your father developed several codes regarding Mara, and Kathryn knew the codes as well," Michelle says thoughtfully.

"Bingo, sweetheart. You have passed Advanced Cryptology Royal Security Level Quadruple Alpha," I say, noting the look of surprise on Michelle's face.

"I will give Susan a comcall tomorrow as I think that Charles is sick again," I say, touching Michelle's arm.

Michelle repeats my gesture, and she says, "I know that you care about Charles. You look very tired, Will."

Yawning, I reply, "You look tired too, sweetheart. Let's get some sleep." And we move closer to each other, and we kiss.

Michelle and I slept for a few hours, and we woke up at the same time, still facing each other in the moon light. "Can't sleep, sweetheart?" I ask.

"No. I want to ask you something, Will?" Michelle asks.

"What would you like to know?" I answer.

"How are you going to do it?" Michelle asks.

"You mean, Mara?" I answer, and Michelle nods, raising her eyebrows in answer.

"She will not suffer, but in the moments before she dies, Mara will understand what it is like to be on the receiving end. What I can say is, that the execution will be by injection," I say, seeing that Michelle knew that I didn't like to talk about the subject.

At this moment, the bedroom comcall unit chimes. I look at Michelle as I answer the call aloud, not bothering to pick up the nearby handset. "What is it?" I ask.

"Mara of Copia is now in our custody, and she has already been treated, as per your instructions, King William. Mara is in transit, on board the 'Kirk' and she will be arriving on Earth at noon tomorrow. Pavlov's Rim is now secured, sir," the duty royal security officer says.

"Thanks for letting me know, and could you please pass on my compliments to the Security Team involved," I say, trying to stifle a yawn.

"Thank you, sir," and the duty officer signs off.

Michelle looks at me closely, and then she moves closer to me on the bed. We kiss and then Michelle asks, "How do you feel now, my love?"

"Much better now, thank you," I say, just before we both fall asleep.

Chapter Nine
Mara's Final Curtain

This morning, the Royal Family joins Michelle and I for breakfast in the recently renovated Formal Dining Room, which has been recently extended and is now bright and airy. It is now part of the informal dining room. Everyone guessed the reason why we were having breakfast in this room. The atmosphere became quite tense, immediately after I announced Mara's detention. I had snapped at Kathryn, and at Charles, and I could tell that both Kathryn and Michelle were becoming concerned, and I knew that there was only one person that could defuse the situation, me.

"There is something that I need to say to you all," I say in a strained voice, and then I look at everyone at the table.

"I have been very rude to you all, and none of you deserved it. We all know that I can be a pain in the arse sometimes, and I know that by saying that doesn't release the tension or justify my behaviour. The main source of that tension will be gone by this afternoon, and I, like the rest of you, was concerned that the Dark Emperor could return in the future. I want to apologise for taking on too much of the huge pressure, it's just that I didn't want a new Dark Emperor to destroy what we have achieved. I had forgotten that you are all here to assist me. I want to apologise to you all, for not trusting you. You know me well enough to know, that your king isn't perfect," I say, placing my face in my hands, and I lean my elbows on the table.

I immediately felt one hand placed on my shoulder, and I instinctively knew that it was Michelle. One of Kathryn's hands is next and considering that I had been so rude to her lately, I knew that Kathryn knew me too well. Everyone is aware of the stress that I am under, considering that I am about to perform an execution. As much as I hated Mara, I wish that I didn't have to kill her, but I know that she could escape again.

Slowly, my tension dissipated to a point where I sit up again, and I look at everyone at the table. Every single face showed concern, and sympathy for me. I notice that Charles is visibly tense.

"Charles, your suspension is now lifted, and I do that on one condition," I explain to a surprised brother-in-law.

"Which is?" Charles asks with some understandable suspicion.

"You are not John the Baptist. If you have a problem with me, I want you to have the confidence to approach me. Don't give me an un-ceremonial bath. I will still help you with your problems, but I need you to show me that you still have what it takes, and I want everyone else to know that. I am not perfect, but you all know what my role is, and I expect everyone to remember that disrespecting me, disrespects the White Commonwealth," I say, watching Charles closely.

Charles, with a look of surprise on his face says, "I will try, King William."

I pick up my coffee cup and I drain the dregs of coffee.

My personal comcall unit chimes suddenly, and I look at Michelle as I answer the call, picking up the unit like a 21st Century mobile phone.

"What is it?" I ask, suspecting the answer.

"Sorry to bother you, sir. You know who has arrived and she

is waiting for you in your private office. Everything is ready for you as requested, Your Majesty."

"Thanks, Phoebe. I will be there soon," I reply, and Phoebe signs off.

Michelle looks into my eyes when she asks, "Mara's arrived?"

I reply nodding,

"Mara has arrived."

Kathryn and Charles nod gravely, understanding the situation and as I looked at the members of the Royal Family seated at the table, Rebecca, and Marina nod at me in understanding and the others gave me sympathetic looks.

"Thanks everyone," I say. And I turn to Michelle, "I will understand if you don't want to come, my love."

Michelle gives me a determined look which reminds me how much Michelle hates Mara.

"I will be there for you, sweetheart," she says. We both stand and leave the formal section of the dining room.

As Michelle and I approach the door to my private office suite. I ask Michelle gently, "Are you sure that you are ready for this?"

Michelle places a hand on my shoulder. "Let's do it, Will," she says, as we enter my private office suite.

We enter my inner office facing the desk. Mara is seated in front of us facing the desk. Michelle and I walk past Mara, and we sit down behind my desk facing Mara, blinking with a light shining in her eyes. I nod, and the royal security guard switches the light off.

Mara was wearing disposable coveralls again and her wrists and ankles were bound with plasticuffs. Mara just sits staring at me.

"Thanks for coming to see me, Mara," I say in a friendly voice.

Mara scowls.

"You are a barrel of laughs, William," Mara says with annoyance and surprise. I knew that Mara's surprise came from not knowing about speaking.

"I thought that you would appreciate history repeating itself to some degree."

A royal security guard enters my office and places a folded-up item on a stretcher that was near Mara's chair.

"I thought that it would be nice to have a friendly conversation with you, and reminisce about the past," I continue in a tone, just to annoy my guest.

Michelle asks me softly, "What are you doing?"

"Screwing with her mind and I hope to get valuable information," I reply, not caring if Mara heard Michelle's question.

"Who are you talking to?" Mara snaps.

"Settle down, Mara, and if you don't, I will carry out your sentence earlier," I say icily, which silences Mara.

"What do you want?" Mara asks and before I can answer, my desk comcall unit chimes.

I pick up the handset. "This is King William."

"Will, you asked me to give you a call at this time," Kathryn says on the comcall unit.

"Thanks for letting me know, I will pass it onto our guest," I reply, sneaking a look at Mara and I sign off. Mara is watching me with suspicion, and she had started to understand that she only had a few minutes left to live.

Staring at Mara, I say, "That comcall was from security. Your friend, the Scrapper never made it to Pavlov's Rim, and he has now disappeared. Apparently, there is a price on his head.”

Mara laughs sarcastically. “Better luck next time, sire.”

I look at the wall clock in the room.

I give Mara a smile as I reach into the top draw of my desk, and I take out a small leather pouch and I place it on my desk. Mara gives me a smug look.

“Have you ever wondered why you have never seen the Scrapper and Enigma at the same time?” I ask her.

Mara shrugs her shoulders.

“You have been led down the garden path. I am Enigma and the Scrapper.”

“Bullshit,” Mara says, glaring at me. Mara says nothing as a stretcher is moved close by Mara’s chair and I stand up at the same time.

Another royal security officer enters the room and walks over to the stretcher. She quickly unfolds a body bag and then stands with the other royal security officer for a moment, and then the security guards walk over and pick Mara up, and place Mara on top of the unfolded body bag and they zip it up slightly.

A medic from the White Palace Medical Service, nods to me and then inserts an IV cannula into the back of Mara’s hand and then looks at me. I pick up the small leather pouch and I carry it over to a table near Mara, while she watches closely.

When I am standing next to Mara, I gesture, and Michelle comes over to me. Mara finally sees Michelle and spits out, “You bitch.”

I unzip the pouch and I take out three preloaded syringes. I look at Mara and hold up the first preloaded syringe so that Mara could see it and Michelle sets up a pulse oximeter and places the sensor on one of Mara’s fingers.

“Mara, you murdered my father, and destroyed the

reputation of humanity, or at least, so you thought. No one in the multiverse believed your bullshit that you said about my father, King James, or anyone else. You have been played like a harp for years by me, and you were stupid enough to think that I supported you and I suspect you killed your father too. Not that I care. Time is ticking Mara and it's time for you, Mara of Copia to die," I say flatly as I insert the syringe into the cannula, and I press down the plunger. Quickly, I follow up with the next two preloaded syringes. I bend closer to Mara, and I say to her as she starts to lose consciousness, "This is for murdering my father. Enjoy death." Mara murmurs something as she dies.

Moments later, the pulse oximeter shows that there is no oxygen in Mara's body, and she has no pulse.

I look at the two royal security guards, "Call the medical officer," I request, and one of the guards steps through the door into my outer office and comes back with the medical officer.

The doctor looks at me expectantly, and I nod towards Mara. She goes over to perform a medical examination. After checking for several minutes, the medical officer says to me, "Mara of Copia is dead, sir." I nod slowly as the guards zip up Mara's body bag and wheel the stretcher away from my office.

Michelle and I hug each other in relief, relieved that Mara is now dead.

Chapter Ten
Ghosts of the Past

I was a bit naive to think that with Mara's execution, my stress levels would return to normal. Even though Mara's body is now in the White Palace Medical Service Mortuary, I was still not happy. No one likes killing another human being, the fact is they stay with you. The rest of the day after Mara's execution, I kept to myself, and I played minigolf to try and stop thinking about how I should feel.

Michelle had noticed how despondent I was. I was sleeping even less than before. When I couldn't sleep, I would go into our apartment's sitting room to watch a 4D vidscreen comedy, as Michelle needed her sleep, and I fall asleep in our sitting room in my favourite recliner chair. Eventually, I would wake up and I would go back to bed and sleep soundly for the rest of the night.

Michelle and I talk about it, and we were both glad that I had taken a few days off after Mara's death. I would do my non-urgent boxes to prevent my work piling up and I was looking forward to seeing Queen Noor and Princess Susan, who are coming to the Milky Way for a state visit. I knew that Charles was going to follow up his counselling sessions with Susan while she is in the Milky Way.

From what Kathryn told me, Noor and Susan would be travelling to Centauri with Charles and Kathryn, and they would continue onto Andromeda.

Kathryn, Charles, and Michelle meet Noor and Susan on

arrival at the White Palace Spaceport, so that I could continue to relax. On the morning of Noor's arrival, I was in the informal dining room, working on my last couple of boxes. I was enjoying a large café latte and a ham and cheese croissant as I worked. Doing some of my work in the dining room had become a habit of mine several years ago. My mother Queen Frances had told me that my father did the same thing.

I watch Kathryn, Charles and Michelle enter the informal dining room, followed by Noor and Susan and I feel the happiest I have felt for some time. Looking at the chair next to me, I was pleased that three of the boxes were completed.

Kathryn and Michelle see me watching, and they smile in return as they walk over to my table, with Noor, Susan, and Charles. Everyone notices the clutter on the table, and I indicate with a nod that it is OK for them to sit down.

"Sorry about the mess, I decided to finish my boxes here today, while I enjoy my coffee and croissant," I explain.

Noor replies with a grin, "I do it myself, Will."

I look at Michelle and she nods her encouragement, so I turn my attention to Susan.

"Susan, I take it that Michelle told you about the sleep disturbances that I have had over the last several nights?" I ask.

Susan replies sympathetically, "She did, King William. Michelle has told me about the sleep disturbances. What we will do is come back here after visiting Centauri, we will be here for a fortnight before we return to Andromeda, so I will do a session with you then."

Something makes me look towards the main informal dining room doors and I see Rebecca, Ann, and Elizabeth walking towards our table, and I look at Susan questioningly.

"I have asked for Rebecca and Ann to check your vital signs

and Elizabeth will be assisting them," Susan says as I turn my chair to face my cousins as the trio come to a stop, right behind Michelle.

Rebecca starts checking my blood pressure and Ann places a pulse oximeter on my right index finger. Elizabeth was watching my reactions closely, and after a few minutes, Rebecca, Ann, and Elizabeth look at Susan. Rebecca stands on my left and places her right hand on my shoulder.

"How is King William?" Susan asks.

"His pulse rate and oxygen levels are normal, and his blood pressure is slightly elevated, which explains the slight redness of his skin," Ann says.

Rebecca looks at my face, and then faces Susan. "I agree with that. The king's face is redder than normal, but considering the recent stresses that he has experienced, I am not surprised," Rebecca explains, as she puts her hand on my shoulder again, this time giving a reassuring squeeze.

"Cousin, are you able to recall anything from the sleep disturbances?" Rebecca asks me, with her hand on my shoulder still. I knew that Rebecca was concerned.

"I keep having this recuring dream where I am being tortured by Drago again and again, which changes into a vision of my father's death," I say, my voice straining slightly. Rebecca pats my shoulder again in reassurance.

Susan looks at me thoughtfully. "I will do a quick counselling session this afternoon with you, sir, and then again, after Noor and I return from Centauri. You have a form of PTSD which is easy to treat. Just continue to take things easy."

"Thanks, Susan. I appreciate it," I say.

Susan looks at the mess on the table, with screen pads, paper notes, government boxes, scattered across the table. "I like the look of the table," Susan says with a grin. I look at Kathryn and Michelle, who smile back.

Susan asks, "When was the last time that you and Michelle, had a real vacation?"

"We were at Vega eighteen months ago," I answer.

There was a commotion in the Lounge area of the informal dining room, and we all turn our attention to the nearest 4D vidscreen on the wall. I look at the nearest member of my personal security team, and the vidscreen is immediately activated and onscreen is a MW4HD Newsflash caption, 'Mara of Copia is dead.'

A News reporter is onscreen, saying, "Today, the prison asteroid containing the former Dark Emperor, Mara of Copia, the daughter of the former Dark King, Rasputin, was destroyed in a collision with Oumuamua, the interstellar comet that passed through the Earth Solar System back in the 21st century or in the year 2017. An official statement from the White Palace will be made soon, but it is understood that King William has stated in an official statement announcing the incident as tragic and that sensors in the region report that the prison asteroid was destroyed. The king has asked the Galactic Navy to assist Mara if she has survived."

The news reporter pauses briefly, and then says, "I can confirm that Mara of Copia's body has been found drifting in orbit around the mysterious Oumuamua by a Galactic Navy IGAL starship and an autopsy has been performed by the medical officer on board the Valiant already. Findings are yet to be released. The decision has been made for Mara to be cremated immediately and her ashes scattered in space."

I look again at my security team and the vidscreen near my table returns to standby.

Everyone looks at me, nodding slowly.

"I will contact Madeira and see when we can visit," Michelle says.

"Thanks, sweetheart," I say.

Michelle hugs me and says quietly in my ear, "Well done with operation snowjob. You're best yet."

I look at Noor and Susan, who both nod as I finish my now, cold coffee.

"Does anyone want some coffee, we could relax for a while, which will allow me to finish this box," I suggest and Kathryn replies,

"I will order coffee for everyone."

I look in my box and there was one thing left; a single sheet of paper, 'Mission Accomplished – The Shadow' is the title on the first page and I place it in the destruction box. I place the now empty box and the destruction box on top of the three finished boxes, and then look up. Michelle and Rebecca smile, knowing the last major after effect of the fall of the Dark Empire is now over.

Rebecca says to me quietly, "Remind me not to piss you off, cousin."

"It was for both of us, Becky," I say, looking across the table at Charles.

As Kathryn returns with a servbot that has the coffee, I say to the group, "Finally, we can start to relax. Please remember that this was a Royal Quadruple Alpha Security level operation. Noor and Susan have been involved for a long time with this too." I look at Noor and her sister. "Thanks guys," I say, as everyone has a sip of coffee.

"You're welcome," Noor replies.

After lunch, while Michelle and Kathryn look after Caroline,

Susan, Rebecca, and Ann join me in the sitting room of my private office. I sit facing the others and on the coffee table in front of me, sits a mug of English breakfast tea.

"I think that the catalyst for my sleep disturbances is the fact that I really did not want to execute Mara at all, but as king, I knew that my duty is to the people that I serve, and I couldn't take the risk that she escaped a prison asteroid again. I admit that I would have preferred to exile her from this galaxy entirely and set her asteroid on a course that would have taken her to Dante's Galaxy in about 12.5 billion years travelling at 100,000 km/s," I explain.

"You and Michelle would have passed Dante's Galaxy on the way out to where you found the 'Wanderer' on the Swordfish mission," Rebecca asks thoughtfully.

"That's right, Rebecca. We used Dante's Galaxy as a waypoint for the trip to the parking location of the Wanderer near the Milky Way," I said, pleased that my cousin remembered.

"Cousin, I have always looked up to you, and I have always admired your dedication to duty. Even when you have been terribly busy, you have always been available to help others, especially me," Rebecca says.

"You're welcome, Becky. Always," I reply. Rebecca blushes.

I have a sip of my tea as Rebecca adds, "Many people look up to you, Cousin William, and they acknowledge your service career in the Galactic Navy. You lead us all with honour and poise and many people, especially me, owe our lives to you. You have done things that have cost you dearly."

And then Ann says, "You are an inspiration to us all. We are enormously proud of you, and we know that you try to have fun when you can."

Susan says nothing as I look at both of my cousins. I must look like a rabbit caught in the glare of car headlights. I start to smile, encouraged by the kind words of both of my cousins. "Thanks, Ann, and thanks, Becky. You are so nice to me, and I honour the both of you too." Susan watches silently.

Susan, Rebecca, and Ann exchange glances and then they look at me again.

"You are making excellent progress, King William. The PTSD comes from several contributing factors such as your service in the Galactic Navy, your duties as presiding monarch as well as being the Golden Sceptre in human form. It is obvious that there are misgivings about your destiny to merge with the Golden Sceptre or you could still be trying to process the merger," Susan says carefully.

"What about Mara's execution?" I ask.

"That's the sense of duty, and the realisation that you can finally grieve those that have lost their lives," Susan says sympathetically.

Susan looks at me with a grin on her face.

"Don't forget that you owe me a minigolf game," Susan says looking straight at me. I look at my cousins and start laughing.

"Who me?" I ask.

Susan nods, looking at me.

I look at a nearby clock and I see that it is only three thirty p.m.

"Why don't you ladies join me for refreshments in the informal dining room?" I ask.

"Only if you are buying," Rebecca says grinning.

"That's why it is beneficial to be a cousin of the king," I say to laughter from Rebecca, Susan, and Ann.

We stand up, stretching our legs and arms and then we leave my office suite together.

Epilogue

Over the weeks and months that followed, I had finally started to let go of the negative feelings that have constrained me for years and I was no longer worried about the Dark Empire returning. There would always be some form of threat to galactic, universe and multiverse peace.

Regarding my counselling with Princess Susan, Queen Noor's younger sister, I found the sessions helpful, and I was making sure that Charles was working through his long-term problems, caused by exposure to CovZlay.

I am working extremely hard to make sure that the Council of Crowns retains relevance in a changing environment, and I was pleased that the younger members of the White Commonwealth Royal Family were doing everything that is required of them too. We always make sure to catch up over a meal or a coffee and have fun when our schedules allow.

The great thing is that my own health is improving too. I play minigolf regularly, and I walk to get fresh air regularly, and Michelle is becoming clucky because of several babies in the royal household.

One late afternoon in late spring, Michelle and I were walking through the White Palace grounds after we returned from a state visit to Copia, Centauri and Sunev. We sit down at a picnic table, drinking from our water bottles.

"Will, if the situation between you and Mara was reversed, do you think that you would have turned out differently?"

Michelle asks, knowing that I was still a little sensitive about Mara. I must have glared at Michelle quite harshly, but I knew that Michelle's question was fair enough, so I answer,

"Yes, my love. More than likely, and I am sure that she would have executed me if she were in that situation. Why do you ask?"

"I know that you have been thinking about this for years, so could you please do something for me?" Michelle asks nervously.

"Certainly, sweetheart," I reply.

"You don't have to keep watching out for her any more, and if there is a future threat to peace in our galaxy, we will meet it together," Michelle says nodding.

In the distance, I can see Rebecca walking slowly, and I invite her to join Michelle and I. She nods gratefully and sits down after a late finish at the White Palace Medical Service, and I could see that she was wearing her gym training gear.

"Becky, is everything all right?" I ask with concern for my cousin.

"I had a double shift, but I decided to go for a walk as soon as I got home from the hospital. I felt like having a nap, but I decided to go for a relaxing walk before I eat and return to my apartment," Rebecca says with a yawn.

"Feel free to join us for dinner tonight, Becky. My treat," I say.

Rebecca hesitates slightly, and I knew that she was thinking that Michelle might object.

"I need your input on something anyway, Rebecca. That way we can kill two birds with one stone," I say.

"Only if I am not intruding, cousin," Rebecca replies.

I look at Michelle and Michelle says, "Please join us,

Rebecca. I know how much Will values you. Sorry, Will and I were talking about something earlier, and I think that this is what Will wants your input on," Michelle says, realising that Rebecca had misread her body language.

Rebecca brightens considerably and she smiles. "Always happy to help my favourite cousin," Rebecca says.

"Thanks, Rebecca. I will briefly go over what Michelle and I were discussing," I say and then I explain the main points of my discussion with Michelle.

"As much as I disliked Mara, I never actually hated her, and I suppose that is the reason why the days following were not plain sailing since Mara's execution. I am certain that if our positions were reversed, she would have had no hesitation in killing me," I say to Michelle and Rebecca.

Both women exchange glances, and Michelle asks, "What do you mean, sweetheart?"

"Mara wasn't a complete idiot, and from what Praetor Augustus said to me recently about Mara's childhood that was spent on the Zherk home world, which was governed by his father at the time. Mara was sexually abused for years by Praetor Caligula, once he knew that Mara was only partially human," I explain. "Please don't get me wrong, while I am sympathetic to Mara because of her childhood, I also know that Mara made a conscious choice to kill her own mother, which started Mara's downward spiral, and when she started manipulating her father, Mara's transformation into the evil person we knew, was completed," I say to Michelle and Rebecca.

"How long have you known that?" Michelle asks.

"I actually suspected most of it," I reply.

Rebecca looks at me closely. "Do you mean that is why you carried very heavy burdens during the Dark Times, which explains why you took charge of things. It was to protect us all," Rebecca says thoughtfully, cocking her head slightly.

"That's right, Becky. We may as well, have an early dinner now. I will talk more about this later," I say as I stand up and Michelle and Rebecca do the same thing. "There is to be no shop talk during the meal," I state, and both Michelle and Rebecca agree. We start walking to the entrance of the Royal Apartments.

In the time that Michelle was secretly placed in Mara's household, Michelle found out that Mara didn't hate me either. We both had a job to do.

I am incredibly grateful that I have such an understanding family, and it takes an understanding family to assist with the various transitions in life.

As a combat veteran, my family knew that I had been through hell, during my service in the Galactic Navy. I could have died many times over, but my skills, intelligence and drive got me through many times. In my early service career as a pilot, my callsign was 'Fox' because I was cunning as a fox and other pilots dreaded drawing me in competition but valued me as a partner in combat.

Even though my career was guided by the Council of Crowns and my father as king, no one realised that I was the heir to the White Kingdom throne, however senior officers panicked when they realised that the future king was a battle toughened combat veteran, and the Council of Crowns assured the officers that is what I wanted. I understood that we needed to prepare for peace by preparing for war.

My graduation class was intrigued as to why the king, members of the royal family and the Council of Crowns were present at the ceremony, and the next day, I started working as an intelligence officer, and I continued to serve in the Galactic

Navy at the same time.

I admit that I had to do horrible things as part of my service, and I also worked secretly with the Shadow which was a quasi-criminal and military intelligence unit that quickly had to evolve and expand through the universe, and I became known to Sanctuary and Vega for different reasons. They already knew that I was the Golden Sceptre in human form and the Larip outside our time confirmed this.

In the last stage of my life, I know that I will merge with the Golden Sceptre, and I was no longer worried. Thanks to the Royal Family, I have all the support that I need.

Time will continue its relentless march onwards, and I know that I am as ready as I will ever be, facing my destiny.

The End of "Sanctuary: Destiny" by Gavin Catt
Book Five in the Sanctuary Series.

E Mare Libertas (From the Sea, Freedom)

Other Books in the Sanctuary Series:
Published by Olympia Publishers

Prelude to Sanctuary (Book One) by Gavin Catt
Sanctuary (Book Two) by Gavin Catt
Project Genesis (Book Three) by Gavin Catt
The Dimension War (Book Four) by Gavin Catt

There is more Science Fiction from Gavin Catt Coming Soon.